T0197481

To order additional copies of this book, contact:
Xlibris
844-714-8691
www.Xlibris.com
Orders@Xlibris.com

ISBN: Softcover   978-1-6698-2337-7
        EBook   978-1-6698-2336-0

Print information available on the last page

Rev. date: 05/02/2022

Mer

Venus

Earth

Mats

Written by **Fiona Dixon**
Illustrator: **Imtiaz Durrani**

Saturn

Fiona, The Doctor in Space

Jupiter

Mars

Neptu

The Universe
is so big,
and learning
about it will
be amazing.

One thing I know for sure
is that I like to help people.
I like animals, and I like
learning about outer space.

I like learning new things
because I am going
to be a scientist.

Doctors help us stay healthy!

AND

Outer space looks like so much fun!

Imagine being so close to different Constellations. What a day that will be!

I know about the eight planets: Mercury, Venus, Earth, Mars, Jupiter, Saturn, Uranus, and Neptune.

There are Dwarf planets in the solar system too.

Pluto, Makemake, Eris, and Haumea are some of the Dwarf planets

Neptune

Uranus

Saturn

Sun

Jupiter

Mercury

Venus

Earth

Mars

Dwarf Planets

Pluto   Makemake   Eris   Haumea

Sun

Remember the sun is
a star NOT a planet.

Did you know that there are over 100 billion galaxies in the universe, and we live in the Milky Way galaxy?

Umm,
I love milk!

I will take care of people and sick dogs and cats on Mondays, Tuesdays, and Wednesdays.

On Thursday, Fridays, Saturdays, and Sundays, I can go to space to help astronauts who are not healthy and cannot return to Earth. I can help them stay healthy.

Monday Tuesday Wednesday

Thursday Friday Saturday Sunday

If they have a little puppy with them, I can help the puppy too, so that I can get some more money, then my mission will be complete.

Additional Helpful Information: NASA refers to Astronaut-Physicians or Doctors as "flight surgeons" specializing in caring for our astronauts.

Cool Fact: Mae Jemison is the first African American woman in space who was also a physician and flew on Space Shuttle Endeavour's in 1998.

Printed in the United States
by Baker & Taylor Publisher Services